What Happened When I Stopped Watching TV

Alec West

Hierophant Writing and Art • Matthews, North Carolina

This book is a work of fiction. Names, characters, places, and incidents are products of the author's imagination or are used fictitiously. Any resemblance to actual events or locales or persons, living or dead, is entirely coincidental.

Hierophant Writing and Art

Published in the United States.

ISBN: 978-1-944591-59-5

www.supposedcrimes.com

This book is typeset in Goudy Old Style.

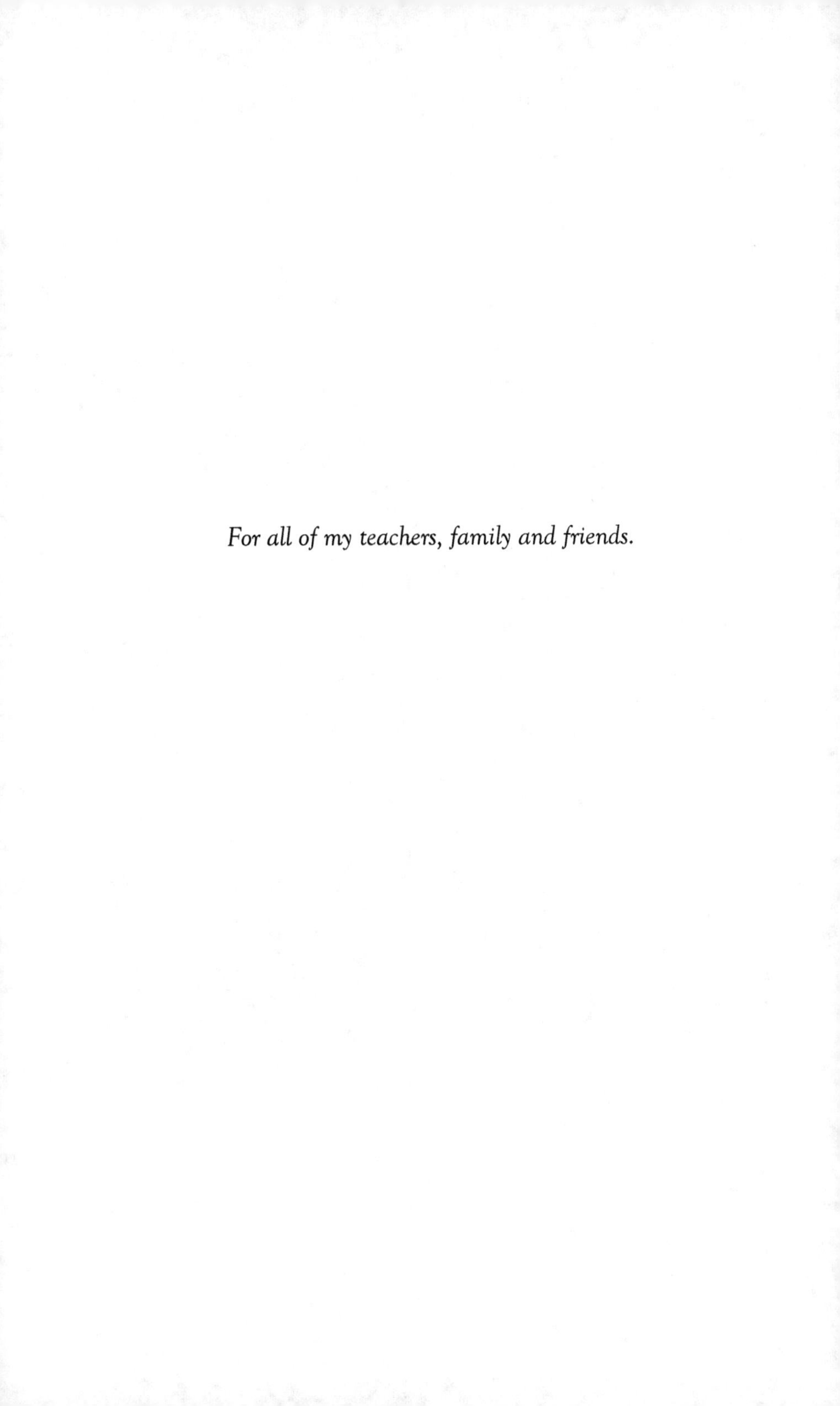

For all of my teachers, family and friends.

Trigger Warning: This book contains detailed depictions of sexual assault, child abuse, incarceration, drug addiction, psychotic episodes, suicide and other traumatizing events.

Table of Contents

What Happened When I Stopped Watching TV

Kid Scissors

HER FACE APPEARS LIKE A VINE IN MY PATH THAT COULD NOT BE PUSHED BACK, SMILING, GLEAMING IN THE SUN.

"So, what's up." She is unassuming, sweet, but behind that facade looms a sinister intelligence, an intelligence she has had to cultivate like an unmarked pack of seeds in a sandy patch of soil. I grunt, stammer and stutter something. I spent ten bucks on a few hits of hash from the only cannabis club I know that serves underage kids without medical cards. Measure Z clubs, pot clubs not legal but overlooked by law enforcement. I was high, dog-paddling through this reality. It was all I could do to focus on what she was saying, much less utter a response.

After about thirty minutes of "Breakfast with Blockhead," throughout which she was texting on her phone, she says, face pure and sinister as ever,

"Do you want to meet my friends?"

"Ok." My brain wants to be somewhere else, but she's pulling me back into her painfully bright world with claws like a cat's. My body, still blossoming into a young man, wants girls, but my brain, stoned and foggy as it is, just wants more drugs.

We move into an American-style diner. Two serious-looking boys about my age sit at a table eating french fries drizzled with barbecue sauce. I introduce myself to them. One's name is easy for me to process, it goes into my mind, out of my mouth and out of my head. The other one's name I still remember. It was harder for me to understand so I made him repeat it.

"Di-an-te." His eyes are white, he is scowling at me. He is angry that he has to repeat himself, that he has to spend his time meeting me. I sit down with her and the two henchmen, and we are all silent.

"Do you want anything to eat?" I ask. We are here on the pretext of a date, after all. She refuses with the utmost politeness, still beaming and gleaming with a sweetness that rots my teeth.

The other two scowl, anger staining their faces. I stammer for a second, wheeling backwards in my mind for something worth saying. Finally I land on the one thing I've been thinking about the whole time I've been texting her.

"Do you know where I can find some LSD?"

"He just wants drugs," says one of the henchmen.

"I don't know, try the park," she says, referring to the People's Park, a shabby paradise of little things in plastic bags.

"Oh, ok."

"Bye." She beams, they scowl, I stammer, pack up and leave.

Where else to go but the park?

At the center of a sun-struck clearing sits a man with wide, watery eyes and shaky hands. He pulls the shining white tabs out of his simple backpack. The golden hour of the day when the sunlight casts a red-orange hue over everything between branches of trees. He cuts the tabs over the crotch of my pants with a pair of kid scissors. He seems only half-aware of what he's doing; the other half of him is in that sunny somewhere else that has been part of the geography of Berkeley since the early 1960s. I buy one tiny piece of white paper smaller than my pinky nail for ten dollars, put it between my gum and my lip, and begin to see the world through a fish's eye. What's dead ahead of me is clear, but my peripheries are unfocused and swirly, as though I'm immersed in a glass bowl of water. The world erupts with a shimmering light, as though diamonds are floating on the wind in a sheet of misty rain. I walk home and see women wearing flowing white dresses holding wreaths of flowers over their heads, dancing in circular patterns while a black-bearded man on an old Southern porch sings opera.

It is springtime; I am on acid. Not LSD but acid, and I become aware of that the next day during French class. I sit at my high school desk and feel the burning corrosion coursing through my veins, the mind-warping effects receding like a wave of the ocean leaving me washed-up, writhing on the beach like a crab or a baby sea-tortoise, belly up. My body is pulsing with heat that cooks my insides. There was something in that acid. Of course there was. There always is.

This is a painful memory of being dissed by a girl, of not knowing what to do once I found her. Our connection was wasted, and I became aware of how inexperienced I was. Yet it is also a happy memory of striving, of getting high on a weekday night in the dawn of my true teenage years and the freedom therein. It was a good day. I swam through the deliciously polluted waters of the old Bay, the Bay I remember from growing up, before the tech boom, when a seventeen-year-old kid really could buy acid on the street and witness a Berkeley ritual of springtime, and everything would be fine.

Overheard Conversations

INSOMNIA,

the last few nights have been
really rough.
Every time I wake up, it's bad.
White noise machine, dude.

What we're training is that repeatability
So you can have something that feels like a race
I really want to win all the time, or I'm not gonna ever win.

Go to school or go home or go to the mall or something
(The whistle while you work song from *kill bill*)
Can you help me save it?
No, you should have asked me that earlier
So the cancer spread from his jaw down to his shoulder...

People don't like me.

You're all messed up.

Excuse me, do you have any cheesecake?
Yeah.

There really needs to be a total take-over.
Some are getting it, and some are not.

When a plane flies close to the sun, does it burn?

No.
Why not?

Because the sun is too far away to burn an airplane.
But it looks so close.
That's because it's very big and very bright.
So airplanes don't burn when they fly near the sun?
No.

El Sabor

My friend, Red Raindrop Esperanza, wrote the word "love" in black spray paint on the corner of Eugene and John street.

He wrote it underneath a bush, dark green and hairy with red furry flowers that I've only seen in California. Raindrop was from Maryland. He brought a can of spray paint cross-country with him in his backpack. His backpack was stuffed heavy, thick and fat with the contents of his life. He had draped a bright blue and pink scarf around it to offset the gray seriousness of his piece of luggage. The scarf was like a sail, sending him off on his voyage, adding a weightlessness to the heavy quality of his reality. Being homeless was something he fought to have a good perspective on. He wasn't homeless, he was free.

Where I have chosen to stay in my parents' house, eating meat every day and receiving mail including taxes and medical bills, Raindrop chose the life of the officially invisible vegan that his soul yearned to be.

He told me he was on the beach and he saw a man carrying a fat, fifty-pound salmon he had just caught from the surf. Fifty pounds, that's enough for the winter! Caught for free from the belly of the ocean, from the abundant garden of the water, the product of a deep connection with the Earth.

Raindrop wrote "love" on the sidewalk here in California, not the end of his journey but an important stop. He was off to LA, then to Lima, then Iquitos, then deep into the Amazon jungle. From the deep rainforest he would emerge reborn from a shaman's brew, then he would get back on a plane and go to Amsterdam, then Paris to live out the rest of his life with the woman he loved. I was grateful that Raindrop had chosen to stop and see me on the way to completing his transformation.

Raindrop wrote the word "Love" on the day when we ate nothing but half a peanut butter bar. I convinced the woman working the Bank booth in front of the grocery plaza to give me the chewy amalgamation of nuts and sugar. She said she was giving them out only to people who signed up for some kind of home mortgage deal thing that Bank was doing.

The night before, we had used Raindrop's spray paint to draw an image of Ganesh, the remover of obstacles, the Hindu god that reveals the path, the offerer of protection, on Rory's apartment wall. We had had to put our bandanas over our faces because the fumes from our contents-under-pressure cans had made us feel woozy and faint. In our stomachs were burritos and nacho tortilla chips from a taqueria in the Mission called El Sabor. Raindrop got excited when he saw that it was called El Sabor and declared that this was what he had come to the West Coast in search for: a burrito with real Mexican flavor. We dined on that exquisite, sharp, citrus, cilantro delicacy with black beans. Then we returned to North Oakland, Berkeley, Emeryville. The guys at the liquor store encouraged our young female friend, Rory, to get the biggest bottle she could afford. She was not 21, but they were jovial, excited to see this eager young woman get her drink on. I passed out from spray-paint fumes, half a bottle of whiskey, the last of our weed and a day spent walking around the hills of San Francisco.

I awoke lying on my side on a mat on the hard, carpeted floor. Paint particles, like smoke, rise to the top of a room, so if you get down and crawl you can make it out. But I stood too close to the sky, and I fell.

"Mornings after are weird," said Red Raindrop. My head felt like it was made out of clay on a wet day, heavy and sodden with whiskey. We put Rory's weed pipe in a pot of boiling water to release the resin. Then we smoked, lighting the bottom so the rich black goo would evaporate into us. Resin for breakfast, hungry, crowding around the pipe in the bare grass backyard of the North Oakland apartment.

"Ya, that was the most animated sex I've had in a long time," Raindrop said. He had fucked Rory. The jealousy added to the acid rolling around in my gut, but I didn't say anything. I needed water, food. Words echoed through my headache as I began to wade through a swamp of jealousy. It sounded like Raindrop spoke to me through an aluminum drainpipe attached to my head, wrapped around my ear.

"Well, we would have included you, but you passed out, man."

Those nights and the spidery webs of fate and youthful rebellion and sex and art and alcohol and marijuana resin that connected us all have spilled off into the gutter with nothing to stop them.

Every week I walk past that street in Oakland and I see the word "Love" written on the sidewalk, and I miss my friend.

Brick, Brick

1.

I insisted that I was a *brick.* Opiate-crazed I floated, zooming into a dream of a man in a sweater vest with a tie and glasses. He looked like a Harvard professor.

The oppressor.

"And every day, I lay another brick in the wall." I imagined myself underneath the bricks, being bricked-in like the victim in *A Cask of Amontillado.*

Your bricks are the mundane things
you do
in your life
every day.
Taxes
go to the war, go to prisons,
do not go
to the people
struggling
to survive.

Only if I build walls too.

My walls make up my own prison of isolation. Isolation tastes stale and acrid like an old, yellow-paged book. Imagine if it were suffocating the inside of your mouth and bubbling up the back of your throat.

2.

Are you going to be a brick or a window? Can you be a brick through a window of a bank or a corporate office tower or the very White House? Can you be the brick with the message twined to it that wakes someone up out of their slumber with a thump? My Grandma sewed bricks into a quilt, a tapestry of desert animals from the place she grew up. There was a coyote and a snake and a bat and a wild horse with no saddle running as though through a dream. They've been trying to build things out of bricks for years, but remember when we used to run like wild horses through open pastures underneath that big, moving sky? Why can't we get back to that? Don't your legs itch to run again like you used to? Even you, brick-layer

tax-payer, have you forgotten the way the Earth felt underneath your hooves? The way the desert wind whipped your naked body?

Drop a businessman off naked in the desert and he'd think he was fucked. I must have learned those survival skills because I'm still here.

He Can't Breathe Part I: The Principal's Office

He can't breathe.

The kid sitting in the office can't breathe. He took his asthma medication, and he still can't breathe. Like Eric Garner, he's wheezing and choking out words.

"Relax. Relax," I tell him.

The teacher groans when he enters the room. They just want him gone. They talk about him behind his back when he's not five feet away.

When he's gallivanting around the yard, refusing to follow orders, refusing to submit, I feel for him. It's dead for him out there, in here. He has to take his only chance at freedom. I'm not sure if Jason can't control himself or if he knows what he's doing is wrong and does it anyway because it feels good. Probably both.

All I know is that feeling of not being able to breathe, like those nightmares where you want to scream but you can't because the pillow is in your face, smothering you.

I would lash out at people as a child so that they would pay attention to me, so that they would feel me. I had to express the pain that I was in because there was no other way but to transfer that pain onto others. Now there's a boy who is like me and needs help, and I am in a position to help him. No one cares about him, and it's not fair. It's not fair that he has to hit the other kids and there's nothing we can do about it. He needs more help, and he's not getting it. In this way, I'm just doing what's in front of me, to care for a lost, sick boy the way people cared for me when I was a kid.

EVEN THOUGH

I REMEMBER THEM TAKING MY SHOES OFF SO THAT I COULDN'T HURT THEM WHEN I KICKED THEM.

I don't play that song anymore, but as a kid it used to be my theme song. I made people feel bad, and they made me feel bad, and I still feel bad, and I wonder how they feel, but I still loved them. I wonder if they knew.

I didn't know how to control or express my emotions. I just fired them off whenever I felt like there was an opportunity. There was never an appropriate time to be emotional. Sometimes it feels like there never is.

Jason is in the fifth grade. He's the first kid I've ever had to physically restrain. We didn't take his shoes off. There was no one there to do it for me. I grabbed him and held him. He banged his head against my chest, but it didn't hurt.

"You're hurting me!" He shouted.

"I wish there was another way," I told him,

"but you can't hit people."

In a dream, I sat with a woman in all-white, in a rain-soaked marble garden.

She pulled beads of water from the limpid pools and strung them across my chest as she sang in a soft voice.

"The same boy whose body hurts him today is the boy that people used to sit on in storage closets, the same boy who took almost every drug you could name and was lost for a long time, the same boy that people accused more than they listened to.

Those trials live on

in your body and in your mind."

The beads of water melted into my chest,

and the sadness I always felt was something other was inside of me again, sadness for myself and sadness for Jason and all the other kids like us. I sank down. I was tired. I didn't say anything for a long time except,

"yeah...

yeah...

yeah..."

I am a teacher now. Every day before I go to sleep I question. Was what I did today necessary? Did I need to discipline that kid that way?

Every night I accuse myself,

every night I fall down in despair,

and every night I am forgiven.

I'm trying to find the line between discipline and abuse. How do you take care of a child who wants to hurt you and themselves and everything around them? How do you stop them while still holding them with love?

My best teacher forgave me. She forgave me for hurting her with my words and hurting her with my fists and feet. Now that I am a teacher, I know the pain when a child who you have given everything to, who you've sacrificed for, who you love, turns on you and tries to hurt you with no warning and no reason.

It's enough to knock you over.

It's like being kicked in the stomach.

You can't breathe, and you

don't want to get out of bed, but you do,

you go back to work and teach that kid the right way to behave,

the best way to treat people.

My best teacher made me believe that I was a great writer,

that I was intelligent,

that I had value and had something to offer this world.

She found a way for me to get published

when I was twelve years old. When I wrote something,

she asked me to read it to the class, and when I was done she said, "Wow. Read it again."

I made her teaching harder that year, but she always brought me back, kept teaching me as long as she could, because she wanted to, because she loved me, because she cared.

My worst teacher sat on me.

He dragged me into a room with no windows and metal grates on the floor and sat on me

until all the fight was drained out of me. I would lie

there screaming under his weight until I couldn't scream anymore, and I was still,

sobbing quietly.

He would sit on me until someone came to pick me up.

He did this many times, as though he were violently training a dog. I learned later that this is a tactic used by guards in juvenile hall, and even there it is considered abuse.

The same things that are done to young teenage boys in prison

Were done to me in a public school

When I was eight years old.

These practices are happening in our schools, but they don't have to be.

As a teacher's aide, I've had to restrain kids who were being dangerous to themselves and others, but I've never had to do it for very long, and while I was doing it,

I was listening to them.

When you restrain a kid, you have to focus all of your attention on them, letting them know that you still care about them, that you're trying to keep them safe. You talk to the kid, try to get them to calm down, and as soon as they promise you that they won't hurt you,

you let them go.

This is compassion.

This works. This doesn't cause the child pain years later, this doesn't burn the feeling of powerlessness into their psyches and cause trauma that affects their ability to love others and themselves.

Back in the marble garden, she talked about a doctor from a tribe in West Africa. This shaman went to school in England and became a psychiatrist. He took a young boy suffering from schizophrenia back to his tribe to take care of. Among his people, those who perceive reality differently are revered as seers and are surrounded and protected by the community, given the ideal conditions so that they can communicate directly to God.

They create art and music.
They heal people.

My friend Basil used to sing and play the guitar. There's nothing he loved more than riding his skateboard, and it made me proud to see him speed down hills faster than any longboarder. He died of a heroin overdose. His parents put him in Imperion towers.

People were protesting outside the building because there was sewage in the drinking water when we came. We found him wild-eyed in his one-bed room, shaking his head back and forth. He had decided to stop using heroin, but he was sinking into the quicksand pit of all his past regrets. All the monsters that lived inside his mind took up arms against him, sharpening their blades as the sun set and the wave of warmth and protection that heroin provided started receding.

Basil begged us not to leave him to the long night that lay ahead.

We did.

He never made it out the other side.

The doctor from the West Africa brought that kid back to his community so that he could have an experience. He came out of it and found he had greater clarity, insight, wisdom and control over himself, his emotions and his perceptions. There's an idea that illness is something that you have to experience fully, you have to let it overwhelm you, let it wash over you, and come out of it healed, whole.

The room they trapped me in had no windows.
Cardboard boxes on steel shelves
lined the bare walls, and I sprawled on the floor,
red-faced,
screaming,
kicking.
Fluorescent lights,
mundane conversations about real estate,
and a fifty-year-old man sitting on
my back.

In the marble garden, she held me. I breathed in her love and breathed out all of my secrets, all of my guilt, all of the dark things that I don't share with anybody. I breathed them into her. She still held me.

I sit with Jason, and he tells me a story of a haunted house he went into. He is ten years old. He has just narrowly avoided being 5150'd, being taken by the police to a mental institution because of his behavior. He tells me about floors and floors of gore, disembodied parts, human and animal, hanging from the ceiling, writing in different languages on the wall in blood, moving shadows. Loneliness. Fear. New sensations terrible and
Real.

My great grandmother was diagnosed as a manic depressive.

She played the violin.

Do That Again

When you cut my skin, it makes me human.

The pain is my friend. When you lock me in a room until shit drips down my leg, do it again. That's why I act out so much, that's why I pound with my fists. I want you to forget about me. I want your ears to be immune to my cries. I want to feel like I'm nothing, like I'm worthless. I'm fucking tired of feeling loved and appreciated. I'm tired of feeling valuable. My contributions are not that great, and you know it, so act like it. That's why I love you, that's why I always want to be around you, you make me feel like I'm less than shit if I'm not conforming to your expectations.

"Oh, yes Ma'am!"

Take all my glory as an artist and throw me in the dumpster, soiled, throat cut, bleeding, used, abused, never good as new again. I don't want you to understand me, I want you to punish me for not sucking the dick of your massive ego. Fuck you. I'm obliged to suck you off right. I understand that's my job, that's the whole reason why I came to this party, was to find you and let you have your way and then leave me out in the rain. I want you to act like you don't care about me. Even if you do, throw me against the wall. Lock the door behind me. I want you to come back to haunt me when I try to pick up the pieces of my life. I want to be able to say,

"I was having a beautiful evening with my friend until your name came up."

I want to feel like God is punishing me, but you're not God, you're just a drunk boy.

I want my life to get harder. I want to have something taken from me, a facial feature like an eye or a nose, except it's on the inside of me and everyone can see it. I want to be unstable like a house of cards made of concrete, steel and sound so that I can come down crashing because it is more fun that way. Life is more interesting and adventurous when people show you that you aren't shit and you have to prove them wrong to yourself so that you can get out of bed, make a cup of coffee and go to class.

The bus ride in the morning is rainy and full of cynical, cigarette-smoking hipsters in bright orange beanies and denim jackets, and everybody knows the most horrible trauma of your life. I want that to happen again, but with feeling, really put your energy into it this time, God, or whoever you are, and I really hope you don't interpret this as a prayer because it scares the shit out of me, and lately you've been answering my prayers.

Different Kitchens, Different Friends

THE REFRIGERATOR MAKES A SOUND THAT MOST PEOPLE DON'T HEAR.

My friend Charles grew up on a boat and said that when he had to live in a house he hated the refrigerator. It was so loud, it kept him up at night. He wasn't used to it.

My friend J used to come over and raid my fridge. He showed me how to cook tortillas on the stovetop. Years later, he admitted that he'd had a gun on him in our house. Old friends were trying to kill him, and he had to protect himself.

My friend Basil also used my kitchen. He is dead now. I remember him standing in my kitchen, having a conversation with my Mom about yogurt-coated granola bars.

"These are actually sweeping the nation as one of the best new things!" he said. His wide eyes were shifty and unfocused, his blond, box-springed hair was like a brillo pad under a wool cap or a hoodie. We went on that afternoon to get drunk in an alleyway with fresh green grass growing. It was springtime, and we were enjoying being young and the bold, deep flavor of loneliness when you have someone to share it with. Then Basil bought a bottle of vodka from a homeless man with my money, and we blacked out in the bathroom of a drug store.

This kitchen, on Lake in Piedmont, by Beach Elementary, was the first place I discovered alcohol. I remember coming home in a nice button-down shirt from the freshman dance and finding the liquor cabinet open.

Vodka and Gin. I filled up two plastic water bottles full, one red and one blue. My friend Red covered the stairs at the Morcom Rose garden with orange, green, white, and yellow puddles from the paints in his stomach. They were inkblots spilled over a page. Somebody was holding their pen up too long thinking about what to write and splotches ran through. Back then there was less loneliness than hope and excitement. I felt like I could still be part of something here if I tried. Red was my first drinking buddy.

Years later, I find myself in my brother Gabre's kitchen in Eugene, Oregon. He has liquor bottles displayed above the cabinets where he keeps plates and dishes. He was a teetotaller all through high school, and now that he is in college, he is drinking. He felt that he had earned the privilege with his success. My friends and I taught him all about top shelf bourbon and scotch.

Now he is a connoisseur and a snob, and at six pm on a weeknight he is shaking the cocktail mixer, fixing a drink.

My friend Hombre's Dad's kitchen looks out over the whole of San Francisco. You can see the city shimmering with light and heat and fog and silver and gold during the day and shining with purple and orange at night. It was the perfect place to enjoy a blunt with some close friends. My friend Hombre had sixteen pot plants growing on that back deck in high school. At first, his Dad didn't notice, then he didn't care.

Tall, fragrant bushes, sticky flowers and phosphorescent leaves. Orange hairs, white hairs, purple hairs. Acid and mushrooms and looking at the clouds. Hardcore music. Drum and bass music. Dubstep. "A State of Trance."

We found a vast, dark basement full of all flavors of

people who did drugs in San Francisco, from hardened criminals to kids like us. Hombre wanted to wear sweat pants and a Nine Inch Nails T-shirt. We told him to go for it, but he didn't do it. We were too young for ecstasy, we felt, so we took trucker speed, those pills you buy over the counter at the gas station for like five bucks. That and a lot of marijuana, and we didn't sit down for six hours.

All this is what I remember of my childhood in the East Bay. What were we gonna do?

We were making the best out of a teenage situation in suburban California. No, you're too young to get into the club, but there's this alley way and this bag and this homeless guy who agrees to buy you alcohol. I'm not joking when I say that homeless guy became my best friend. His name was J, he was only a few years older than me, and he taught me a lot.

This Kid is a Soldier Part I

J PULLED OUT A BOTTLE. STICKING OUT OF THE PAPER BAG, I SAW A DRAWING OF SEAGULLS AND SAILBOATS ON IT.

"What are you drinking?" I asked. He didn't answer. He put the bottle away after taking a swig. We didn't speak that day, but talking to Biff and Boff later, two kids from the local park, they said he liked me, he thought I was chill.

"Somebody called me?" Somehow I had J's phone number. I don't know where he was living at this time, but he didn't have his own place of residence and wouldn't for a long time.

J was about five years older than the rest of us. He had a thick, pink scar on his nose as though it had been split open. He said he had been robbing a house with his friends when the cops pulled up. He heard the siren and jumped up so fast his nose broke on an open cabinet door above him. Getting to the hospital was a blur of blood, pain and fear of getting arrested when he was already on probation. Or maybe he didn't go to the hospital. Maybe that's why it scarred like that.

"What's that scar on your shoulder?" I asked J one time.

"I got shot," he said. "I came out of the apartment complex like this." He made a motion of pulling out something tucked behind his waistband and swinging it up over his head. "And I spun backwards. I woke up in the hospital with a note from a detective on my chest." We were in a hotel room with white flakes on the table and he was trying to impress a girl. "Whatever you do," he said, "don't get shot." He took a swig of whiskey. "It hurt like a sledgehammer knocking into me." He had to have titanium pins surgically implanted in his shoulder to hold everything together and get it working again. He said he stretched to wake up in the morning and was met with searing pain as his pins slipped out of place. He needed surgery to fix the damage, and that was the end of his days as a carpenter, mixing concrete for six hours straight and building patio decks for rich people. He was left with very few viable options for making money except for the one obvious one, the one he had always known.

J was always a drinker. Of the two types of alcoholics: bingers and all-day-drinkers, he was an all-day binger. Where some people drank all day with sips from the flask, he did damage to fifth bottles of whatever kind of liquor he could afford as he went about his day. He would stare lovingly at an empty bottle of cheap rum bigger than his arm and say, "You did that!" Proud of himself and how drunk he could get.

He was proud of me too.

"This kid is a soldier," he would say. "He's smart and he's loyal. He takes the things that I say, and he learns things from them. Then he learns things from those things."

Other people saw me as awkward. They didn't understand my motivations and didn't want to hang out with me. I had very few friends during that time but a lot of acquaintances, a lot of urchins who stuck to me and sucked my life away with false promises and harsh disappointments. Not J. J was a real friend. J was there.

Our crew of chronic-smoking, drug-dabbling teenagers even staged an intervention for me. People who would never invite me into their homes all of a sudden cared so much about me.

"You shouldn't fuck with that cat, breh." They said. "You could get shot chillin' with him." It was true. J had multiple warrants out for his arrest and was wanted dead by people he used to deal drugs with. Where most of us were from Piedmont or Berkeley, J was from Oakland. Deep East Oakland. He had sold drugs, he had stolen cars and he had gone to jail and prison. He said that, on and off, he had spent three years of his life incarcerated or detained, and he was always afraid of going back. We rolled together, scrounging up whatever we could find and spending it all on whiskey, weed and fried chicken from the grocery store.

Riding in his car one day, J knocked me on the head with his pack of cigarettes and told me,

"Don't do no cocaine. You're too smart for that."

He told me that if I wanted to be noticed by more girls, I needed to clean myself up, wear fresh pants. "And when I say 'fresh,' I mean brand-new 'fresh.'"

Not the dirty-work pants I always sported under a scary t-shirt, portraying to the world that I didn't care at all. *Stop smoking so much weed by yourself and being so stoic around other people. Talk. Tell jokes. Don't shoplift from stores because it's not worth going to jail, trust me.*

These are lessons I've carried with me, that have served me well, that nobody but my Mom ever tried to teach me. People thought I was weird, thought I was fucked-up, and they let me do my thing. Without a community to show me the right way to live, I got arrested. I walked around trying to impress girls without any result or any idea why it wasn't working. I was suffering, alone and desperate. J reached into my world and told me to snap out of it, and then he helped me. He helped me build confidence, which is the best thing a friend can do.

Don't just pat a friend on the back and tell him he's doing good, show him how he can get better so that he can get the things he wants. I value friends who hold me accountable, friends not afraid to tell me what is and is not working. I want friends with honor, morals, integrity and courage, and despite the warrants J had out for his arrest, he had those.

Urchins

THIS IS FOR THE THINKERS.

My friend Red Raindrop Esperanza said, at 18, that verse perfectly described me. An urchin allergic to his own stinger. An urchin, eyes clouded with resentment. An urchin, a pile of blue-black, baggy, dirty, ripped clothes like you might find next to a gutter. An urchin allergic to his own stinger. Someone who steals, someone who manipulates, someone who scorns the respect we show to others as members of the same community in favor of drugs.

Raindrop and the wonder he shone with was around at first, but they left as the air turned chilled, threatening the first snowfall of winter. It would be a blizzard year. He didn't want to deal with it. He returned to where he was from, and I was alone in a community of cold shoulders. I had one other friend, but he lacked Raindrop's ingenuity, passion and sense of wonder. He just wanted to do drugs all the time, he just wanted to drink and do drugs. He and I grew very close.

I remember when some kid gave us an amount of money, forty dollars, to go out into Santa Fe and buy fungus, the kind of fungus that grows on old rotten fruits in your kitchen, the kind of fungus that makes you grimace in dismay when you pull your bread out of the bread bag to make a sandwich for lunch.

Their bag was bought and passed around a car full of fiends. What remained of their investment when we returned it to them was not enough, not enough.

I got high that night, but I didn't get invited to a lot of parties afterward. Everyone around me rode up a mountain in a warmly lit gondola, clinking martini glasses and listening to pop rock hits. I walked down a slushy road with wide, dead-set eyes, my muscles aching and sore from cold and intention on the nights that I did sleep. Get high. Feel something. Feel nothing. I passed out tearful, singing to the ones who weren't there, splayed out on top of my bed or curled up into the covers around my shaking self.

An urchin allergic to his own stingers, not a thinker as much as a feeler.

I wanted to be loved, but I didn't know where to begin with that. The kind of love I needed had never been shown to me before. It was the kind of love that makes you feel supported, that makes you feel like you're worth something. I buried my face in the snow, letting my hands numb and my nose run red.

All I knew were the things that you buy from men in cars. That was the closest I'd ever been to the feeling I wanted to have. It wasn't the same. I needed to be able to see myself in a mirror that forgave. Tired of holding myself up by my own strength, I longed to be supported and to show others that I could support them. I pushed my two mattresses together, side-by-side, and longed for somebody to share the second mattress with me. People saw me, but they kept their distance. Distance was the only thing I kept with anyone else.

I sit on top of the water tower watching the sun set over the purple Sangre de Cristo mountains and the dust devils whirling in the desert far away. I used to pull little pieces of dirt out of the cracks in the sidewalk and put them into my lungs. I used to sing in choirs. I used to do musical theatre, I used to write fiction. I came to class with a black eye and people laughed.

"Sup, Alec, you get punched in the face?"

"Ya," I said.

All this happened at a prestigious college of liberal arts and philosophy. So many philosophy students become alcoholics. People study Western culture in depth, down to its deepest roots, devoting their lives to it, forgetting that Western culture has gotten us nowhere. Americans are not happy. This is why I don't flaunt my intellect, I don't wield my education like a long pink sabre for all to see. The study of classical literature hasn't brought me any meaning.

The study of philosophy hasn't helped me move, helped me love, and I don't know if it really helps anyone. While you sit in your ivory tower reading great books, people are starving and dying, and so are you.

I'll carry these wounds for a while yet. I know I've done wrong, made mistakes, fucked people over, and I understand why they did what they did, but the pain is still there, and it runs deep. Horrible things happened to me, and the places where I grew up echo back in time, changing shape but remaining the same. Through time, I'm screaming, through time I'm not being held. I'm still eight months old like I'm still eight years old like I'm still eighteen and it all runs together, years and years later.

"yeah...

yeah...

yeah..."

This is for the urchins with no stingers.

Fuck you.

BURD

I REMEMBER AFTER BASIL DIED, WE DROVE AS FAST AS WE COULD THROUGH THE BERKELEY HILLS AFTER SUNSET.

We spilled beer off of a cliff. We wanted to write his name somewhere. Old Bull Lee said that an unreleased Kurt Cobain song had been put on YouTube the day Basil died. The spirit world buckled and shifted, making room for his body to leave his ghost and go rolling on through the dirt. Most people at his funeral didn't care. They laughed and joked and drank beer. I wrote in the memory book how Basil liked the book *Siddhartha*.

"Is that a book about Buddha?" I asked him one day between Creative Writing and AP English class. We had driven his Swedish Family Vehicle to my house for a lunch of pills left over from my last surgery and some colorful weed I'd bought at a Measure Z club. That was the day he showed me how to jimmy the lock of my parents' liquor cabinet with a butter knife. His hair was free without a beanie holding it down, his eyes were sad, but they still had some light in them. He was not a junkie yet.

"No, Siddhartha is not Buddha. He finds Buddha and follows him for a bit, but then decides to go his own way." I was amazed by that, not his description of the book but how excited he was by it. He seemed to be burning with energy somehow. This is a moment I'll always remember because he was showing himself to me. Happy. A joy to be around.

Intellectual. A good friend.

Understand that at that time, there was hardly anyone else. Deep depression, like a black sky moving slow across a landscape, followed those eventful afternoons in the kitchen. We all drifted away from each other, Basil,

Hombre, until it was only I and Old Bull Lee smoking weed and walking in the rain, hitting a long succession of voicemails on our phones. The world was definitely happening somewhere else. Still, when others weren't there, sometimes, Basil was. He was there, for me, he was there. I could tell him I was sad, and he would listen and then he would give me advice and it was comforting.

Basil dropped out of college. Didn't want anything to do with it. He was brilliant, one of the most outspoken students as we discussed classical literature senior year of high school, but college and the life that supposedly came after it wasn't cut out for him. Many kids are like that. He came back home and worked, but his heart was in pain and his mind was confused. He got into drugs and found himself outside of his family's home. With drugs came guilt at mistakes he'd made, innocent people he'd hurt. I didn't understand, at that time, how guilt can drag a person down, grind you into nothing, make you wish you weren't there.

Basil was on my mind as a nagging worry, like a pain in the roof of your mouth, before he died. *I should call him,* I thought. *I should hang out with him.* Yet some combination of feelings kept me from dialing the numbers on my phone. It was a mix of fear, resentment and just not wanting to hang out with someone who was so depressed. I had gotten sober, I had started doing things with my life, why would I want to hang out with somebody who wasn't like that? Now the sore has opened, and all the pus is dripping down the back of my throat. *Why'd you have to go?* I tried to push him away, to forget about him, but Basil and the past we shared is a part of me, and it always will be. In those times, those aimless, cloudy times, he was there. He wouldn't want me to try to drag myself through the mud for him. He wants me to live. He wants me to go back to sleep, but I've slept too much already. He knows what that's like. He told me he would lie in bed for thirty hours at a time. That was what he called meditation. "You can really think up some shit," he told me.

One full-moon night I found myself back in the old neighborhood where we all used to get high and laugh together. Driving down those streets I can still see him skidding around a corner on his skateboard, so fast I might hit him, his arm perpetually in a cast, a heavy black t-shirt cloaking his skinny frame. I called out his name in desperation, his full name, and I got a response. A wave of sadness with a little piece of love at the core, like a warm rain that leaves you shivering. The darkness deepened. *You still remember me. You were my friend.*

Plants communicate with each other through chemicals. When you smoke weed and feel high, when you eat a carrot and feel healthy, that's the plant communicating with you, sharing what information it has. So it was with Basil and I.

Now I do my best to take care of myself and my friends. I resent some of them too, the way I resented him before he died, but I hold them close. I'm changing as a person, but I'm no different than I ever was. My roots will always be pacing around in the dark, exhaling smoke and laughing.

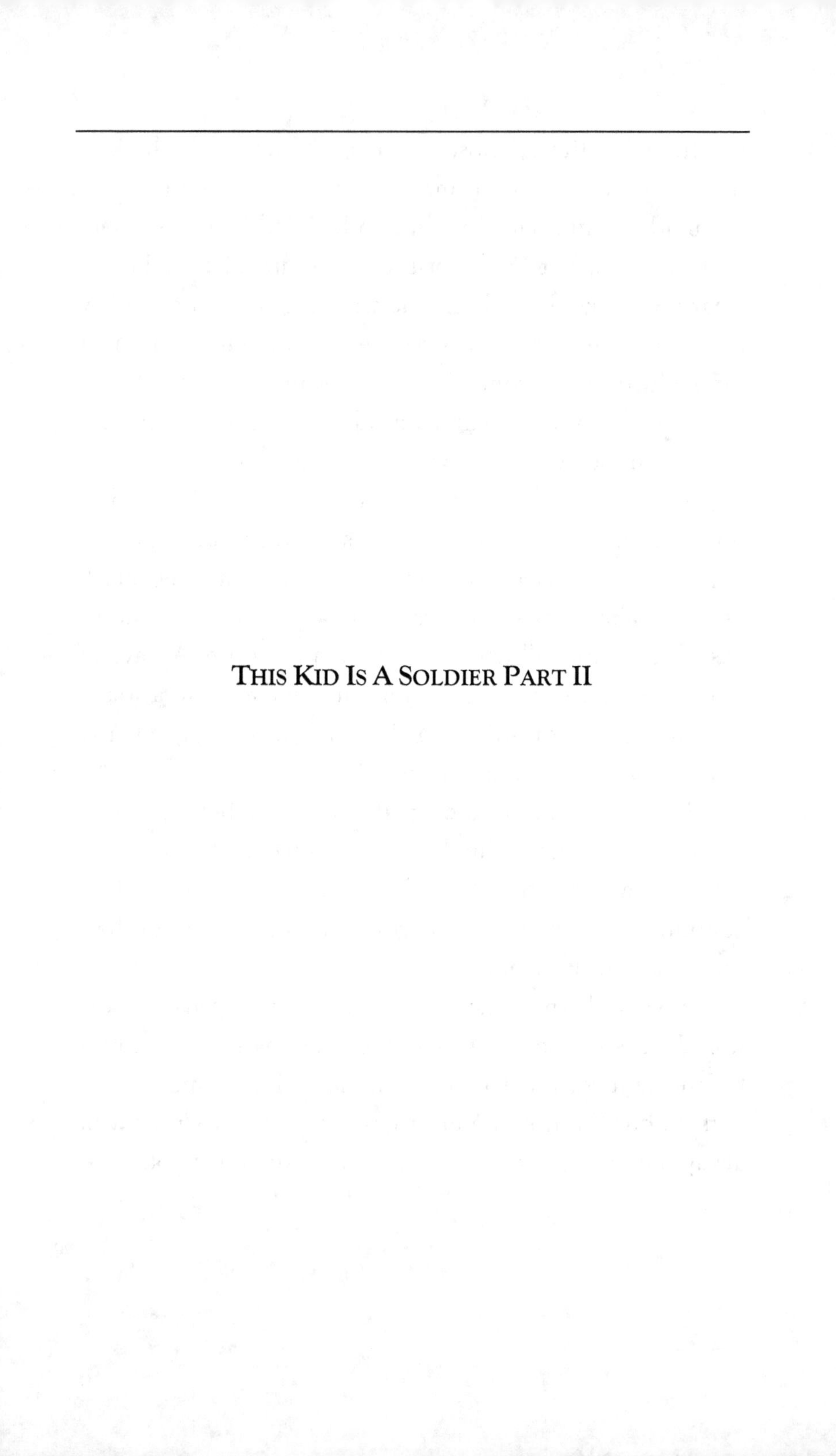

This Kid Is A Soldier Part II

"OH, FUCK," J SAID AS WE GOT OFF THE FERRY AT JACK LONDON.

He was disgusted. Jack London Square in Oakland is a nice, shining, shopping and working area. Fancy, proud of itself, self-righteous. All this was carved out of West Oakland around the port between the freeway and the waters of The Bay. Millions of people live around this Bay, all walks of life, rich, poor, every background and nationality, every religion and way of thinking. We live here and disagree on a lot of things, but we are united by the feeling that this is a great place to live, and a lot of that feeling comes from the feeling of being by the water.

The office towers and restaurants by the water had shining, clean walkways and grass manicured down to every blade. The rocks along the water were covered with many dumpsters' worth of trash. The message from the smoked glass complexes was clear: *We care about how we look, but not about the Bay, not about Nature, not about anything pristine and beautiful, not about anything that matters to you.*

J got off the boat and got right to work. Scrabbling across rocks half-drunk, he started pulling out trash and throwing it onto the sidewalk. Shrugging our shoulders, our other friend, Old Bull Lee, and I joined in. We bent our backs for forty-five minutes, picking up everything that could harm a seal or a seagull and throwing it on the sidewalk where the lawn manicurists could pick it up in the morning.

"Ya, this is really disgusting. I'm finding needles," J explained to a passing dog-walker, his furry dog's hair newly brushed. "And it's really immoral that this walkway is so clean and yet the water is so dirty. You know, people are making all this money, it's time to give back. I mean, you hire people to clean the sidewalk, but you can't clean *this* too?"

The moon moved in the sky, and we called our work done. We had transferred the mess from the rocks and the water where people could avoid it to the sidewalk where people had no choice but to interact with it.

"Ha!" J said. "I bet we could sit down on this bench with that bottle and a blunt, and if the cops came we could be like, 'We did this.'" We would have gotten arrested for public drinking and littering, but we basked in the satisfaction of a job well done, feeling like we had just done something good. We needed to do something good. We hadn't been given a chance. Our roles were relegated to consuming things out of bottles and bags, getting by how we could, waiting every day to get arrested or shot, trying not to think about it. We had to show that we were good people, that we cared, even if nobody cared about us.

It's worth noting that J is doing good now. After years of homelessness, he saved up enough to buy his own property. He became a caretaker for an old man who lived on the coast. Before the old man died, J bought his house. Now he wakes up every day next to the ocean he loves, walking down onto the clean beach that he owns. J has three dogs, three cats, two goats, a girlfriend, and a baby boy and girl. He's living his life the way he always wanted, the way he always knew he could.

I'd love to give this story a happy ending but I can't. J is still tormented by guilt and anger about things he did in the past and things that were done to him. He yells at his girlfriend and says it's a step up from his own step-dad, who used to beat the shit out of him with anything he had on hand. J doesn't talk about prison, the things he did to get there or the things he did to survive while inside, but he's not proud of any of it. He's a good man who's done bad things, and guilt is the worst pain of all sometimes, when you believe you will never be forgiven.

Forgiveness is healthy, but it's hard to learn. It means accepting that the past can never be any different. Maybe the future can. It has to be.

He Can't Breathe Part II: Special Day Class

IMAGINE YOU WERE LOCKED IN A ROOM WITH TEN SCREAMING BABIES FOR SIX HOURS A DAY.

What if those babies were ten years old? What if they were tearing each other apart and there's nothing you can do and there's nothing you can do and there's nothing you can do, and they won't stop and they won't stop and they won't stop and they won't stop, and we need help and we need help and we need help. Under fluorescent lights, the sight of blood feels cold and metallic and stops you dead, and you watch in horror as a shark, or is it a child, delivers the killing blow. You see eight-year-olds smoking cigarettes and wearing orange uniforms and putting tattoos on their faces, and you feel yourself falling down, the ground opening you up, swallowing you whole, darkness closing in as you die slowly, slowly, slowly, over many years.

The school-to-prison pipeline is real. It is a physical thing and you can see it, it's right there in front of you if you look, and I want to shout and scream and tear at the walls around me with my fingernails. It's right there, right here, it's everywhere.

I look at the thousands of people who flooded the streets after Eric Garner died. If every one of those people spent an hour a week in a public school, they would make a difference. We need them to not just go back to their lives when the night is over but to take that love and anger and heartache and sense of injustice and push it into the life of one kid that needs help.

Fluorescent Lights

1.

The room they trapped me in had no windows.

Cardboard boxes on steel shelves

lined the bare walls, and I sprawled on the floor, red-faced, screaming, kicking. Fluorescent lights, mundane conversations about real estate, and a fifty-year old man sitting on my back.

2.

I sit on the window sill of my old bedroom, smoking out of a pipe, blowing the fumes out of the open window. Brown hillsides dotted with green trees. Some times of year, the trees are in bloom, pink flowers with red nipples. I used to smoke pot to connect with music. The Roots. 2pac, Infected Mushroom. Smoke rolling in great dense clouds out of my mouth. Devin the Dude.

3.

The TV in the hospital played *The X-Men*: Rogue, Beast, Wolverine, NightCrawler, Ice-Man, Cyclops. The first time I ever saw *The X-Men* cartoon was before the first surgery I ever got. They opened up my skull and pulled the growth out. A glass tube, a plastic rubber mask, noxious fumes. They flavored the fumes for me since I was a kid. I remember bubble-gum flavored anesthesia. I wasn't ready for it. It was too strong. I slept and woke up and slept and woke up and slept and woke up and slept and woke up.

4.

I remember them taking my shoes off so that I couldn't hurt them.

5.

I had to physically restrain a kid for the first time on Tuesday. We didn't take his shoes off, there was no one there to do it for me. I grabbed him above the elbows and held him above the ground. He banged his head against my chest, but it didn't hurt.

"You're hurting me!" He shouted.

"I wish there was another way," I told him, "but you can't hit people."

6.

I want to be done telling this story, but it keeps being told to me. This is why this is happening, this is why I feel this way. Everything I go through, it always comes back to this.

White gown, green polka dots, special socks. I open my eyes and fall back down onto the pillow. My head is heavier than it's ever been. It feels like it's stuffed full of soggy, warm, wet cotton. Plastic tube, metal needle, strange liquid feeding into my arm. White walls, pink walls, fluorescent lights. Why is so much violence done under fluorescent lights?

7.

"Can I rent *The Goofy Movie?*" I ask my parents after Children's Hospital Oakland put staples in my head. Not stitches, staples. Staples that had to be removed with a staple remover and no attempt at any kind of anesthesia. Who thinks of these things? How does this make sense? The Children's Hospital. A violent place. Alameda Unified School District. Oakland Unified School District. Piedmont Unified School District. Auschwitz. Pelican's Bay. Guantanamo Bay. The School of the Americas.

"Take his shoes off!"

8.

I remember lying face down on the grass in front of my therapist's office. There must have been eight therapists standing around me with five holding me down onto the grass. Grand Avenue cars zooming by. Why did I get so angry? The windows at Ace Hardware across the street were tall and dirty. View inside the store was obscured by the backs of wooden shelves. An ad for a lawn mower, or was it a barbecue, with the word STX.

9.

I don't know if I've ever wanted to jump out of a window. I don't think I have. It was never that bad. Other things happened that I'm not ready to talk about. Prescription pill bottles, orange translucent, white caps, yellow writing. Butcher knife with a black handle and a long, shiny blade. Kitchen counter. Christmas Eve. New Year's Eve. The Oscars. The Super Bowl. TV holidays, always on Sunday.

10.

Our neighbor said she would use a serrated knife next time. That way, even the paramedics couldn't save her.

The Wildest Ones Are Vanishing Quickly

I HAVE APPLE CIDER VINEGAR IN A SPRAY BOTTLE. I HAVE A BANDANA AROUND MY NECK.

I have a pair of laboratory goggles meant to keep chemicals out of your eyes. I have a pair of barbecue gloves because tear gas canisters are too hot to pick up with your own hands. Everything I wear is black.

They have visors. Military grade gas masks. Military grade helmets. Military grade batons. Military grade Tasers. Military grade pepper spray, which is not meant to be used at close range. Their gloves have metal in the knuckles. Everything they wear is black.

My Grandpa is in hospice care.

Happy Veteran's Day.

My Grandpa spent a winter in a cave he dug himself with Nazi grenades, surrounded by frozen Nazi corpses. My Grandpa, who knows the ringing in the ears that comes after a bomb blast levels a library

and how that hollow tin sound mixes with the agonized screams of his friends. My Grandpa, who gave Private Snow the morphine himself.

Let me tell you about the saddest look I ever saw on anyone's face.

Jamie is famous for,

"What the vultures fail to understand is that their attempts to squash our struggle will only embolden it."

Jamie, who was locked in solitary confinement for three months without charge. Jamie, who the grand jury sought to coerce testimony from about the May Day riots.

Jamie. In silence we roar.

The saddest look I ever saw, when I walked out of the room instead of walking with lions. I missed my chance to join with the pride and take all of our freedoms back together, because they were going to come and hunt us all down anyway, and we'd better roar and rip with our teeth or just slink back to our caves and try to die in our sleep. The look was one of pure, innocent sorrow.

You never know how many people are watching you grow.

Lions, more like Black Panthers, more like a pack of wolves because they're taking out all the wild ones if they can. Shooting packs of wolves from helicopters so that cows can graze.

My friend Red Raindrop Esperanza, years after he wrote the word "LOVE" on Eugene and John St., was locked up two weeks for being a street medic during the Baltimore Uprising. A street medic is someone with basic first aid, first responder, or EMT training who goes to protests and demos wearing a black cross patch on their shoulder. In Baltimore, they were assessing head injuries and pouring bottled water in the eyes of tear gas victims when they were caught in the sweep.

There were no guards in the unit my friend Red Raindrop Esperanza was thrown into.

There was a door, and on that door was the imprint of a shoe, and next to it was scrawled,

"Kick the door, pussy!"

If you kicked the door, the guards might come. The others in the unit told him that they raped his friend. They also told him that they respected them both for fighting for their beliefs against the cops.

There was no way to keep the towel on your face. You had to put a towel on your face and do a sit-up. If you couldn't do a sit-up with the towel on your face,

"It's fight night."

When the towel fell off your face, you were presented with a rank 350-pound man's ass and balls, and the fight bell went,

"Ding-ding."

My friend Red Raindrop Esperanza still has PTSD from that event.

On November 9th, 2016 he wrote, "Fuck you too, America."

Future Alec, I want you to remember how this feels to be powerless at the hands of a fascist dictator, knowing you have the tools and resources to do something. I want you to feel the way you did when your Grandpa, the soldier, the cowboy, was dying and you felt paralyzed with jaw dropping and you felt anger trapped welling up inside you, infecting you, making you bleed and hurt and burn.

I think about my teeth. Despite daily flossing, the infection in my gums advances. My dentist told me I wasn't using the right kind of floss. Despite the work I do every day to liberate myself and the people I connect with, it seems our imprisonment advances. Should I use a different tactic? Do I need a bigger weapon?

I think back to Jamie. What they did mattered. I've never felt the fear in a cop's wide eyes when you smash them on the head with a wooden stick of your own. I've been so focused on peaceful, long-term change that I've overlooked the idea that violence is necessary sometimes. Martin Luther King needed Malcolm X. What do I need?

You Can't Get Away With Anything

I WAS IN A BOOKSTORE.

I was checking out the zine rack. There was a young woman scanning the shelves too. I was attracted to the patch she wore on her back, which had a winged insect stenciled onto it. I like people with patches sewn onto their jackets. I think that people used symbols on their clothing or on their bodies in wilder times to tell about themselves or their clan. People wore symbols of honor, respect, dignity. A person could read a symbol and learn about them. That was how people fell in love, made friends, spoke without speaking.

"What're you looking for?" I asked her. She was looking for a book. She had found a book. It was a geography coloring book.

"It's time to learn my countries," she said.

"Yeah, I just remembered Wyoming was a state," I told her.

"Geography is important."

"Yeah. There's fifty states." She agreed. I continued to thumb through the zine rack when I noticed the clerk at the store give me a dirty look. It was the kind of look that burrowed deep inside of me with scorn. It was a look that said,

"I don't know what you're about, but I don't like the look of you or what you've been doing since you showed up." I met his gaze. He was a hairy fellow. He had glasses and a pubic hair beard that went down his neck. He also wore a hat, beige, an Irish newslad's hat. I lifted one corner of my mouth to smile at him.

I kept thumbing around, reading, as the woman and her friend made purchases and conversation with the bookstore guy. The record on the stereo was playing Bob Dylan or some similar form of bluegrass.

The record stopped and was not changed. The people left the store, and silence reigned. It was just me and the bookstore guy. I looked up, and he was grinning at me. I looked at more books. This bookstore was made up of one small room with books on three walls and windows on the fourth, to the street. The guy had Japanese pop crime novels, histories of the Spanish Civil War and World War II, outdoor survival guides, biographies of Jewish revolutionaries. Everything was piled all together. There was no form of organization. It was just books on shelves next to other books.

I found a zine within my price range: $2.

I went to the counter.

"I'll give you this for $1," the man said.

"Thanks,"

"So..uh," he said, "I don't know if it's you, but certain people have been saying that you've been stealing shit."

"What? No! I wouldn't do that."

"Well, I don't know if it's you, but merchants, we talk to each other, and they've been saying you or someone who looks like you has been stealing shit." He made a nervous laugh.

"No, man. I wouldn't do that. I wouldn't steal from a bookstore. That's fucked up."

Feelings came back to me from all the times I *had* stolen things and been caught and confronted. It's uncomfortable to be put on the spot. When you're a kid, people try to assert their authority on you and unleash all their pent-up anger with a stern talking to, thinking this is justified punishment. I had been arrested twice for stealing from stores when I was a kid. Now, as an adult, I wanted no part of being labeled as a thief, especially when I hadn't even stolen anything.

"Well, it might not have been you. They said it was a guy like you with red hair and all that. Anyways, have a good night."

I walked out. The night was purple and heavy with muggy humidity. I sweated as I walked up and down hills on abandoned streets back home. It felt like the bookstore owner and I were the only two people alive in the world that night. Everything else was dark and silent, not moving. I had plenty of time to be alone with my thoughts.

I had stolen some shit. From a bookstore. The bookstore that I had just left that night was in Oakland, CA. The bookstore that I stole from was in Olympia, WA. I had stolen a postcard that I really liked by placing it inside of a book that I bought for twenty-six dollars. The postcard had a painting of Malcolm X on it and a quote,

"*We all need more illumination around us. Illumination breeds understanding. Understanding breeds patience. Patience breeds love. Love breeds Unity.*"

Merchants, we talk to each other,

the guy had said. You can't get away with anything.

Hearts Jack-Hammering

Would you break the window of a car to save a dog from suffocation inside?

When you look into the eyes of the smothered canine, what do you see? What is she telling you?

"There's no hope for me" or "Please just let me be free." Because you can. You can break a car window with a rock, a brick, a bat, a piece of concrete. Have you noticed how there's not a lot out there in terms of easy-access projectiles on our sterilized, suburban streets, I mean, there's not always something you can pick up and smash through a window in a given situation. Is someone out there, removing all the things that could be potentially hazardous in a city situation? Where can we find our tools?

I found a can of spray paint in the bushes outside the tool-lending library.

I knew I had been given a gift, an opportunity, a leg-up. I wish I could tell you I used my projectile weaponry. I even had it all planned out.

I woke up at four am with spotlighted imagery playing in my brain of how I was going to spray paint:

"JAIL THE BANKERS, FREE THE 99%" on the window of a bank looking over a busy intersection.

"What would happen if we did that?" Raindrop asked me. He asked with hope and wonder, his voice trailing off into an infinity where our actions on this Earth matter. Maybe our act of spontaneity would be the spark to set flame to a conflagration (I remember that word from my middle school vocabulary quiz: *conflagration*: a massive, overwhelming, all-consuming fire) Soon after our statement was made to the world there would be Molotov cocktails smashing through white house windows, black-masked avengers walking the halls of congress, and C4 planted in the basements of banking institutions.

One person has that power, like the Tunisian street vendor who set fire to himself, starting off the Arab Spring.

We could do that, we could do that here.

With one act of bravery, we could start a revolution.

Seven billion dogs are trapped, suffocating in German Luxury Cars on hot days with no one else around but you

And a chip of concrete waiting for you to pick it up. You could pick that rock up.

You could save that dog.

You and I could go in at two in the morning, riding bikes, wearing masks, no one would know it was us.

We could keep watch the first night, seeing what time the cops roll by, and tag it up right after.

We could be there

And back in my basement in less than ten minutes,

Hearts jack-hammering, hot, sweaty, red-faced, wide-eyed, we

Did that, it happened, there's no

Taking it back. The hardest part

For me, about that is the week

After,

Knowing you did it and it was very public and now

You need to go about your business, with a cold sweat dripping down your neck, hoping they don't

Call you out, they don't find you at your house.

Does it matter?

I think you should go into that situation not caring if you're going to get arrested or not. Go into it knowing that the message, the statement you're making is bigger than you and more effective than anything you could have done from within the system. So many people say, *I'm going to be a lawyer, I'm going to be a doctor, I'm going to be a teacher, I'm going to be a cop. I'm going to make a change from the inside.*

The lone wolf strikes the hunter in his sleep, saving the pack.

A dog released from his confines, no longer suffocating, the animal can free others locked up in paw-proof vehicles.

But if you're trapped inside the car too, then you're trapped inside the car too. You lose your breath and forget why you came. You want to drive the car away, or at least turn on the AC, but you're not the one with the keys, and you never will be.

What happens if you don't break the window?

Nothing. The dog dies sooner, you die later, no one is connected by bonds of love. Nothing changes, we all die in our own little compartments. Maybe the owner comes back just in time, maybe he comes back to a dead, smelly lump of fur. Maybe nothing changes.

What is love? Love is a fire. Love is a bolt-cutter. Love is a brick. Love is what brings you freedom. Love is what the system tries to replace, to make you forget about. Some people have never felt love, but when you do, when you feel it, the results can be explosive.

With the sound of car alarms, you wake up for the first time and see the power that you have to affect someone's life. You run and feel your heart pounding with an intensity you've never felt before.

You just did something that scared you. Who put that

fear there?

The sun beats down as your feet smack pavement.

Let's hope you never stop running.

You matter.

With broken glass, you've made a difference, you've saved a life.

You've fought back against the tyranny of suffocating silence.

Together, we can howl at the sun.

Thank You, Get The Hell Out of Mexico

"PUES MATALO?"

Eddy was walking down the boardwalk in La Paz late one night. The year must have been 2014 or 2015, when the drug war had reportedly engulfed the whole border area in a bloody conflagration. Beer can in hand, Eddy was wandering when he spotted some men hiding in the bushes. They spotted him at the same time he laid eyes on them. This would be one of the scariest nights of Eddy's life. Eddy laughed, swinging his beer around in a comical gesture. He was about to make a mess of his pants. As he continued to creak down the dusty boardwalk, he heard a question posed. "Pues Matalo?" *Should we kill him?*

"No, no, no," replied another of the men. He said it in a laidback way, as though taking my cousin's life were an unnecessary trouble that they needn't bother with. He must have been from La Paz, Eddy thought later, and knew it was okay to leave the drunks alone.

Eddy had been part of the beer-drinking population of La Paz for five years. He had moved there after he had gotten into a scuffle with the Nevada legal system. A dusty, sunburnt judge had told him that if he ever got caught drinking again, not drinking and driving, but just drinking again, he would spend six months behind locked doors in the Washoe County jail.

Eddy was a baby-faced boy, soft inside and out, and he couldn't stand the thought of jail for any amount of time. He was a smart guy, but his Mom had left him for a spoon and a piece of metal pipe when he was six years old. Emotionally, he limped through life, and his feet were swollen twice or thrice their normal size. Red, the toenails in his heart cut into his skin and the wounds got infected.

Eddy got caught drinking again and had three days to present himself to the judge and face imprisonment. He remembered our Grandpa in the courtroom taking his cigar out of his mouth and shaking his head. Grandpa, a cowboy and a war hero who had never drank a drop in his life. How far the apple had fallen from the tree.

Eddy fled to San Diego, where his brother lived and went to school. He had to say goodbye, he said, because he was going to live in Mexico.

"No," said his brother, Bryan, and his friends, "That's a bad idea."

Cousin Bryan and his friends were college sophomores at San Diego State. They didn't have much more in their fridge than half-eaten tacos, hot sauce packets and a thirty-two rack of cheap, beer-pong beer. They were not wise men, but even they knew that fleeing to Mexico when the drug war was raging around the border was a bad idea. Eddy had no connections, no money and no way of getting back. The same kids that might egg you on to jump off of a roof and into a pool were saying,

"No, Eddy, don't do this, it's a bad idea, you shouldn't go to Mexico."

Eddy went. He spent five years there. He told us he would go out onto a kayak on the ocean where it was peaceful. He went surfing and worked at nice restaurants. He spent time really learning about himself. He would go for days without food sometimes, completely out of options, at the end of his rope in a foreign country, beating himself over the head and the back with a heavy, wooden *I'm such a fucking loser.*

The wind picked up on the shores of the Baja Peninsula, five years into Eddy's retreat, and all foreign nationals had to be evacuated. There was a hurricane impending, and it was going to be horrendous, so bad that they anticipated all emergency services would be taxed to their limit. *Get out if you can. Don't worry about where the plane's going. If it's going to the US, get on it.* The hillsides of Cabo San Lucas were dotted with little fires. In disaster-stricken Mexico, neighbors had to band together into militias to survive assaults from marauding thieves and looters. Every fire meant a neighborhood block that was protected by a cadre of people willing to fight for the safety of their families. Baby-faced Eddy wandered through this apocalypse.

"*Thank you, get the hell out of Mexico.*" As he buckled himself into his plane seat, he prayed he wouldn't be sent back to Nevada, but part of him no longer cared.

Escuche

"WHAT SONG WAS YOU PLAYING YESTERDAY?" ARTURO ASKED.

Arturo is about nine, but he has the mind of a fourteen-year-old. I saw him flirting with an eight-year-old girl on the play yard.

"What are you doing out here?" he asked her.

"I'm in the office," she said.

"Ooooh, you a bad little something."

He likes her.

I sat with him the other day while I ate my lunch. He had hit some other kid in the cafeteria, and the teacher told him to sit with me. She expected me to talk to him about his behavior. I was beyond my threshold of wanting to deal with it. I was new at my job, and helping elementary schoolers with disabilities to focus and learn was the most draining work I had ever done. I couldn't do it all day yet. It was my lunch break. I always play music on my lunch break.

"Do you like rap?" I asked him. He started rattling off the names of rappers he knew like an errant machine gun with a stuck trigger and a screw loose. I couldn't tell if he was listening. I played a song called "Thieves in the Night" by BlackStar. BlackStar was a hip-hop group from the late 90s. They were popular in the underground at the same time when Dirty South crunk music oozed through the air waves with its "*Eh umm numm numm, mm de doomm duh duh dummmm!*"

BlackStar's membership was composed of Mos Def and Talib Kweli. Unlike other rappers, who paint a picture of the world around them that they are at the center of like pre-Galilean astronomers, Mos Def and Talib Kweli tell us of a world that they have no control over and can only influence through their rhymes. They are like train-hoppers, watching the world pass by with the uncertain hope that they have picked the line that will lead to freedom.

Arturo stands on top of the bench. He is emulating his favorite wrestler, yelling proclamations of his greatness to lines of plastic-pig-tailed first graders filing back from lunch recess. I think he looks like the baboon from *The Lion King*, holding up Simba over the rock. The other animals do not kneel, only look at him from the corners of their eyes as they pass.

"Are you allergic to peanuts?" I ask Arturo.

"Yeah," he says, sitting down next to me.

"Shit," I say out loud, something I'm not supposed to do at this job. I pull my plastic lunch box out of the bag it was contained in. The glass and plastic are smeared in peanut butter. I know we're not supposed to bring anything peanut to school, so many kids are allergic. It's good peanut butter, but I'd hate to see Arturo rolling around on the ground wheezing, his whole body puffed up like fat being squeezed by a rubber band.

"*The same boy whose body hurts him today is the boy that people used to sit on in storage closets, the same boy who took almost every drug you could name and was lost for a long time, the same boy that people accused more than they listened to.*

Those trials live on
in your body and in your mind."

"I'm allergic to peanuts!" he repeats in a loud, serious voice. I scoot away from him on the bench. Now I am nervous, and he is nervous too. We are being triggered together. The song has changed.

Soon he gets up and goes into the school. His teacher told him to sit with me or sit in the office. Now he is doing neither.

"Shit."

The next day is a new day, a luxury I never had when I was in school. I would hurt people, but once I recognized that what I had done was wrong, I tried to learn from it.

"Tomorrow is a new day, and you're coming to school with a clean slate," people would tell me. That was almost never true. Every time I made a mistake, the weight of all my past mistakes came bearing down on me. Even now, as I learn, I am stabbed with spikes of guilt and regret at every misstep. My teachers knew nothing about forgiveness. How could I learn it?

Arturo asks me what song I played yesterday. He wants me to play that song about the cell phone, the only song that ever plays on the radio. He plays basketball with Ahmed. He runs to the other side of the court to shoot.

He can't even hear the music, yet it's important to him that I'm playing that song. It makes him happy. When I listen to his favorite song, I'm listening to him.

ABOUT THE AUTHOR

Alec West was born in San Francisco and raised on the border of Piedmont and Oakland, CA. He attended St. John's College in Santa Fe, New Mexico but finished at The Evergreen State College in Olympia, WA with a Bachelor of Arts Degree. He has been published in The Green Windows Anthology 2017, Slingshot Magazine and The Anthology of Poetry by Young Americans.

In addition to writing he has worked with youth alongside such groups as The Beat Within, Chapter 510, Corde-Enfants-Haitiens, and Gateways for Incarcerated Youth. He is pursuing his Master's in Education as an Education Specialist. He lives in Oakland, CA with his family and divides his time between the East Bay and Marin County.

www.ingramcontent.com/pod-product-compliance
Lightning Source LLC
Chambersburg PA
CBHW070450170726
48291CB00005B/1681
* 9 7 8 1 9 4 4 5 9 1 5 9 5 *